The Tale of Miss Nettle

Read-Along

STORYBOOK AND CD

Join Sofia and her new frozen friend, Olaf, in this
exciting tale filled with adventure, friendship, and fun.
You can read along with me in your book. You'll know
it's time to turn the page when you hear this sound. . . .
Let's begin now.

Printed in the United States of America

First Paperback Edition, February 2016   10 9 8 7 6 5 4 3 2 1
Library of Congress Control Number: 2015952427
ISBN 978-1-4847-3040-9
FAC-008598-15352

For more Disney Press fun, visit www.disneybooks.com

DISNEY PRESS

Los Angeles • New York

Sofia had just returned from a fun ride on her flying horse, Minimus. She led him into the stables and began to brush his mane. Suddenly, she noticed the amulet around her neck was glowing blue. Sofia knew what that meant. She had to go to the Secret Library!

The Secret Library was a place where the stories had no endings. It was up to Sofia to find out what each story was about and then help finish it.

Sofia rushed to the Secret Library and sat down in the special reading chair just as a book shot off the shelf and into her hands.

"*The Tale of Miss Nettle*? A book about Miss Nettle? Oh, no, what is she up to now?"

The book flew out of Sofia's hands and landed on a stone pedestal, where it fluttered open.

The narrator told of a far-off land called Freezenberg. It was so cold there that snow always covered the ground and no flowers ever grew—until the king's gardener brought a flower called a snowdrop. The flower was planted throughout the kingdom and celebrated each year with a winter flower festival.

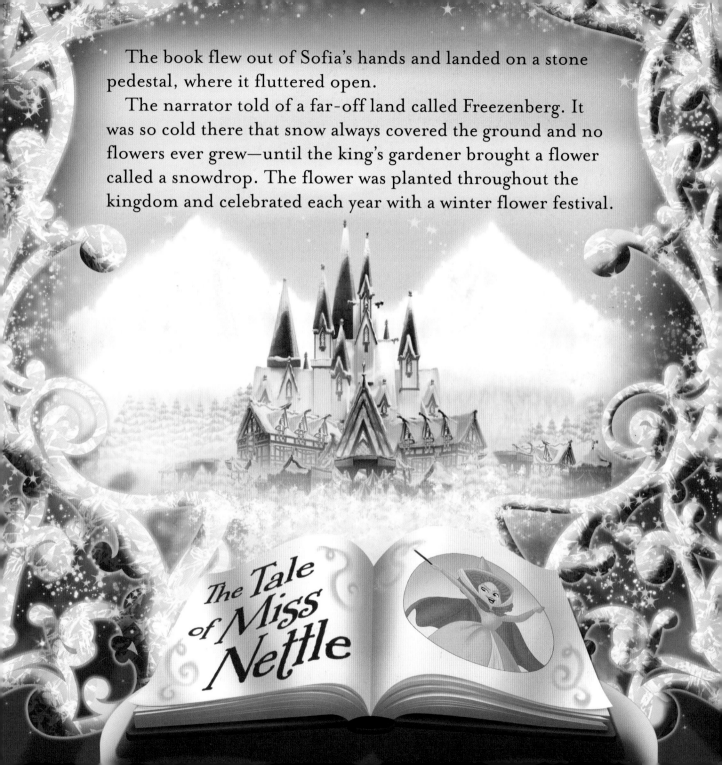

The Tale of Miss Nettle

The festival was to happen that very night, but the wicked fairy Miss Nettle had been stealing the snowdrops. If she took them all, there would be no flowers in the entire kingdom and no Winter Flower Festival!

Sofia jumped up. "I've got to stop Miss Nettle and give this story a happy ending!"

Sofia and Minimus rushed to Freezenberg and soared over the snowy landscape until they spotted Miss Nettle down below. Miss Nettle placed a bunch of snowdrops in her bag. "One flower for me. And one flower for me. And another for me, and—Who am I kidding? They're all for me!"

Sofia and Minimus landed. Then Sofia asked some animals nearby to help by distracting the fairy while Sofia grabbed the bag of stolen snowdrops.

But Miss Nettle *did not* let go of the bag! "Well, well, well, if it isn't my least-favorite meddling princess."

Sofia tugged on the bag. "These flowers aren't yours. They belong to the people of Freezenberg."

Miss Nettle tugged back. "That's what you think. They're mine, and they always have been!"

Sofia didn't know what Miss Nettle meant, but she wasn't about to give up. "I'll find a way to get them back!"

Miss Nettle reached into her pouch. "Not after you have a dose of my crazy crystals!"

Miss Nettle threw a handful of crystals at Sofia. When the magic dust cleared, Miss Nettle was gone—and so was Sofia's ability to talk to animals! She tried talking to the owl and the polar bear. But she couldn't understand any of the animals anymore—not even Minimus!

"My amulet isn't working! It must be Miss Nettle's crazy crystals!"

Just then, Sofia's amulet
began to glow again—but
green this time!

She showed it to Minimus.
"Look! Maybe a princess is
coming to help."
    But it wasn't a princess
who appeared. . . .

It was Olaf, the
enchanted snowman!

"I'm Olaf,
and I like warm hugs."

The snowman looked
around. "Where am I?"

Sofia had a terrible realization. "Oh, no!"

"Ohno, Ohno . . . Nope, never heard of it. Is it far from Arendelle? Because I should probably get back."

Sofia tried to explain the amulet's mistake. "It usually brings a princess to give advice, but a wicked fairy put crazy crystals on it, and, well, it sent you instead."

"The amulet sent me to give advice? I can give you advice." He leaned in toward Sofia. "Don't get too close to fire."

Usually, after giving their advice, the princesses went back home. But Olaf was still there. Miss Nettle's crazy crystals were probably to blame for that, too!

"This is getting worse and worse. Now I need to stop Miss Nettle from ruining the Flower Festival *and* fix my amulet so you can go home."

Olaf promised to help. First they had to find Miss Nettle. So Olaf and Sofia hopped into the sleigh pulled by Minimus and took to the skies.

"Now *this* is the way to travel. Oh, I just love feeling the wind through my sticks!"

Olaf leaned over the side of the sleigh to get a better view.
"Oh, look, a carrot! Oh, wait! Oh, that's my nose!"
He reached out to grab it . . . and tumbled out of the sleigh!

"I'm okaaaaay!"

Olaf landed on a snowy slope and rolled out of sight.

When Sofia looked down, she saw a whole crowd of snowmen
built by children. "Oh, no! Which snowman is Olaf?"
Minimus landed, and Sofia jumped out. She walked down
the row of snowmen until she finally spotted her new friend.

But they still had to find Miss Nettle.

"I don't know how I can stop her without my amulet's magic."

Olaf thought for a moment. "You know, Queen Elsa has all kinds of magic, but it still took Princess Anna to show her how to unfreeze Arendelle. And Anna doesn't have any powers—except that she never gives up and she has a big heart."

Sofia shook her head. "Those aren't magic powers, Olaf."

"I know, Sofia. They're *better*."

Sofia brightened. "Let's go find that wicked fairy!"

"Here comes one now." Olaf pointed in the distance.

"No, that's just my friend Hildegard! Hildy!"

Hildy was surprised to see Sofia . . . and her talking snowman!
She told them her father, King Henrik, was canceling the festival,
since the snowdrops were almost gone. The only flowers left
were in the Royal Gardens near the castle.

Sofia turned to Olaf.
"Wherever there are flowers,
we'll find Miss Nettle!"

A short sleigh ride later, they arrived at the Royal Gardens. Sure enough, Miss Nettle was there. Sofia tried to explain to the fairy how important the flowers were to Freezenberg.

"I'm not *stealing* anything. I'm simply taking back what was mine."

Then Miss Nettle explained that *she* had been the one to create the snowdrop flower—and that the royal gardener had stolen it from *her*!

"But if you take all the snowdrops, there won't be any more flowers in Freezenberg."

Miss Nettle shrugged. "Too bad for them." She waved her wand and vines sprouted up, trapping Sofia, Minimus, and Olaf.

"No!"

Then the fairy plucked the very last snowdrop in the kingdom. "So long, Princess. Tell your Freezenberg friends to think twice before they meddle with Miss Nettle!"

Sofia struggled to break free of the vines, but it was useless.

"At least that fairy got her flowers back. Now maybe she'll be happy."

Sofia realized Olaf was right. "I'm supposed to make sure this story has a happy ending. For everyone—including Miss Nettle."

Olaf separated into different parts and reassembled himself next to Sofia. "Don't be sad, Sofia. You almost made a happy ending."

That was when Sofia noticed Olaf was free. "Quick, untie us!"

Sofia and the others rushed to the castle to find King Henrik. When Sofia explained that it was the royal gardener who had stolen the flowers from Miss Nettle, the king was shocked.

"If she created the snowdrop, we certainly owe her our gratitude."

But how would they get Miss Nettle to return now that she had all the snowdrops?

Then Olaf noticed something. "She didn't get *all* the flowers. She missed this one right here. I noticed it a minute ago. It must've gotten stuck in my snow when I rolled down that hill."

"This is perfect. We can use this to get Miss Nettle to come back." Sofia turned to the king. "Don't call off the festival yet, Your Majesty. Just tell everyone to gather here and wait for me."

Sofia and Olaf jumped into the sleigh, and Minimus took off with them to find Miss Nettle.

Before long, they spotted her. "Come back, Miss Nettle! You left one snowdrop behind!"

Once the fairy heard that, she turned around and followed Sofia straight back to the castle.

When they got to the throne room, King Henrik addressed Miss Nettle. "I understand that you are the very talented fairy who created our beloved snowdrop. We all owe you a great deal of thanks for giving us so much joy for so many years."

The king and all who were gathered began to applaud.

Miss Nettle loved every second of it. "Thank you, thank you so much!"

"So, Miss Nettle, do you think you can give Freezenberg back its flowers?"

King Henrik continued. "We'll only accept the snowdrops back on one condition: that from now on, instead of calling them snowdrops, you let us call them Nettledrops."

Miss Nettle was touched. "Nettledrops . . . oh, take them all! And just to make things even more fabulous, *voilà!*"

She waved her wand, and the flowers began to magically glow and change colors.

Miss Nettle landed. "Thank you for all that you did, Sofia."

"You're very welcome." Then Sofia looked down at her amulet. "Can you fix it?"

"Of course I can!" And with a wave of Miss Nettle's wand, Sofia was able to talk to animals again.

Now that Sofia's amulet was fixed, Olaf could return home. Sofia thanked the funny little snowman for his help. "You reminded me that having a big heart and never giving up are more important than having magical powers. That's just about the best advice I've ever gotten."

"I guess it *was* pretty good, wasn't it?"

Sofia gave Olaf a big hug good-bye . . .

and then he disappeared.

King Henrik and Princess Hildegard joined Sofia. Then Hildy handed her friend a beautiful bouquet of Nettledrops.

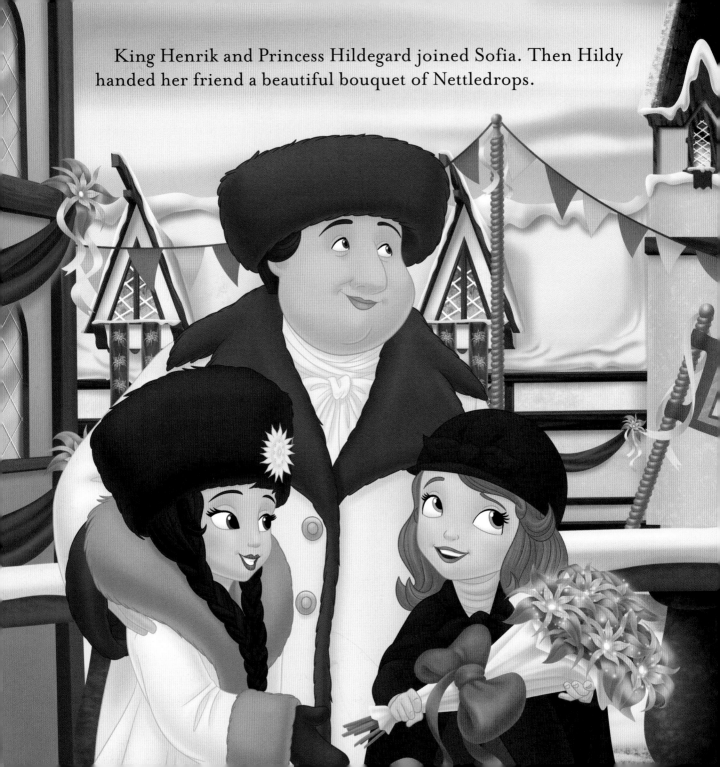